MICE AT THE BEACH

MICE AT THE BEACH

HARUO YAMASHITA
PICTURES BY
KAZUO IWAMURA

WILLIAM MORROW AND COMPANY, INC.
NEW YORK

Copy 1

The last day of school was over. Mama Mouse walked the happy little mouse children home.

Daddy Mouse hugged them. Then he counted to make sure all the little mice were there. One. Two. Three. Four. Five. Six. Seven. Yes, seven was the right number.

Mama fixed an after-school snack. "Tomorrow," she said,
"we will all go to the beach."

"Hurray!" cried the little mice, and they began to show
how they would swim and dive and ride the ocean waves.

What busy little mice! How would Mama and Daddy
keep track of them at the beach?
Daddy had a plan.

They blew up seven small water tubes, and Daddy tied
a string to each of them. The tubes would keep the little
mice safe in the ocean.

Everyone thought the water tubes were great fun.

The next morning the mouse family got up early and
climbed on a train that would take them to the beach.

The train was crowded. Daddy counted several times to
make sure all the mouse children were there.

The beach at last! The day was fine, but the beach was crowded.

"Let's look for a quieter spot," said Mama.

"A good idea," said Daddy. "We will never be able to keep track of our little mice here."

They walked until they came to a calm inlet. There was no crowd, and there was lots of space.

"I will climb up on that rock," said Daddy. "I will watch everyone from there."

Soon the little mice were swimming in the sea. There was paddling and splashing and falling in the water. One little mouse even went fishing.

Mama stood on the beach. Daddy was the lifeguard. He
held on to the water tubes.

Then it was time for lunch. They drank orange soda and ate on driftwood tables. Everything tasted delicious.

After lunch everyone took a nap. Mama and the mouse children fell asleep under the wide umbrella.

Daddy stretched out on the big rock. The sound of the waves soon lulled him to sleep.

They slept and slept.

Suddenly the little mice were awake and shouting, "Look! Look! Daddy's way out in the water!"

It was true. While they were sleeping, the tide had come in.

"Swim, Daddy! Swim in!" the little mice called.

"I can't," said Daddy. He looked embarrassed. "I don't know how to swim."

The little mice wanted to float a water tube out to their daddy, but Mama stopped them.

"Daddy is too heavy for one little tube," said Mama. "And it might not reach him. We must think of something else."

Mama had an idea. She tied five water tubes together to make a raft. Two of the little mice would pull the raft out to Daddy.

The rescuers paddled hard. Soon they were close to the rock.

"We've come to save you, Daddy," said the first little mouse. He was out of breath.

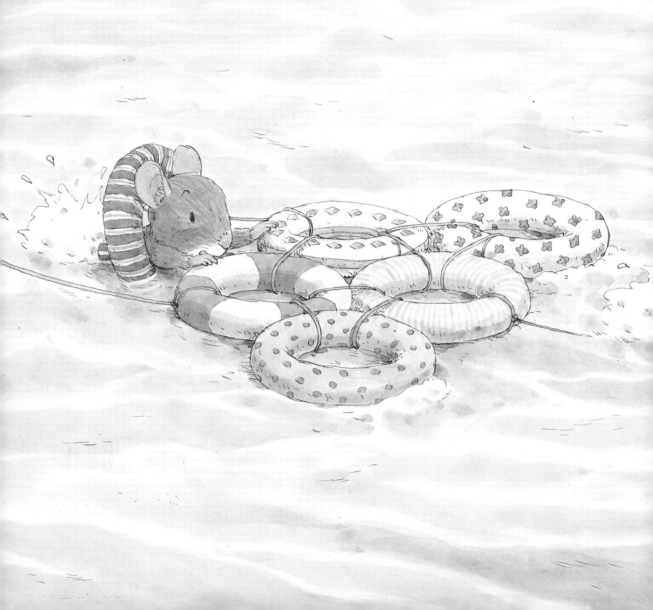

"You're doing a
good job," said Daddy.
"Thanks."

Heave ho! Everyone helped pull Daddy in. "We saved the lifeguard," said Mama, and she smiled.

Daddy was sorry he had scared everyone. "I was so busy keeping track of my little mice," he said, "that I forgot to keep track of me."

In the train going home, the mouse family
grew sleepy.
   Mama stayed awake to count and make sure all seven
little mice were on board—and a daddy mouse, too.

Library of Congress Cataloging-in-Publication Data
Yamashita, Haruo, 1937–
Mice at the beach.
Translation of: Nezumi no kaisuiyoku.
Summary: Daddy Mouse is so tired from keeping track
of his seven little mice at the beach that he fails to
notice the tide coming in where he is taking a nap.
[1. Mice—Fiction. 2. Beaches—Fiction] I. Iwamura,
Kazuo, 1939– ill. II. Title.
PZ7.Y1916Mi 1987 [E] 86-23713
ISBN 0-688-07063-9
ISBN 0-688-07064-7 (lib. bdg.)

JP/*STORY*   copy 1
Yamashita, Haruo
  Mice at the beach   10.25

DATE DUE	
JUL 1 6 1996	
AUG 2 8 1996	
JUL 7 - 1998	
JUL 1 7 1998	
MAR 2 6 1999	
JUL 1 8 2000	
JUL 3 2001	
AUG 3 0 2001	
MAY 2 0 2002	
SEP 0 3 2002	
GAYLORD	PRINTED IN U.S.A.